JUST MY DAD & ME

By Leah Komaiko • Illustrated by Jeffrey Greene

 A Laura Geringer Book

An Imprint of HarperCollinsPublishers

NOTE: *This is a fantasy. Children should never go into the water unsupervised and should wear proper equipment while snorkeling or deep sea diving.*

Just My Dad & Me

Text copyright © 1995 by Leah Komaiko

Illustrations copyright © 1995 by Jeffrey Greene

Printed in Mexico. All rights reserved.

Library of Congress Cataloging-in-Publication Data

Komaiko, Leah.

  Just my dad & me / by Leah Komaiko ; illustrated by Jeffrey Greene.

    p.   cm.

  "A Laura Geringer book."

  Summary: When other family members infringe on what she had hoped would be a special day with her father, a young girl imagines herself alone with fish that take on familiar appearances.

  ISBN 0-06-024573-5. — ISBN 0-06-024574-3 (lib. bdg.)

0-06-443562-8 (pbk.)

  1. Fathers and daughters—Fiction. 2. Family—Fiction.

3. Fishes—Fiction. 4. Stories in rhyme. I. Greene, Jeffrey, ill.

II. Title.

PZ8.3.K835Ju   1995   94-18688

[E]—dc20   CIP

                                                      AC

Typography by Tom Starace

Visit us on the World Wide Web!

http://www.harperchildrens.com

For just my dad,
and the Howdy Doody ranch
—L.K.

For Elsie, Walter, and Anne,
who understood the best
—J.G.

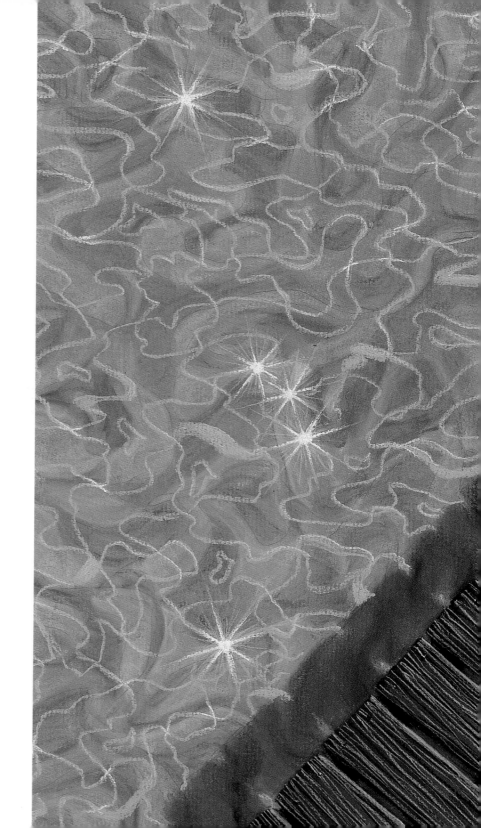

I'm going out to sea
Just my dad and me.

Just Dad and me
and Aunt Monique
and Grandpa Bob
and Grandma Dot
and Grandpa's dog.

Now here comes Mom
she's bringing dozens
of uncles and great aunts,
now here come my cousins.
They *all* want to go out to sea.
With just my dad and me!

I'm showing Dad how I swim.
Only me and him.
Only me and him and
my brother Len,
my brother Lon,
my sister Lee.
I wish that they'd all go away
but everyone just wants to stay.
Now things with Dad won't be the same,
So let's play the RAGS FOR SALE game.

Then Dad takes my hands.
Mom holds my feet.
Everyone quiet!
Now three times repeat:
"RAGS FOR SALE!
RAGS FOR SALE!
RAGS FOR SALE!
WHO WANTS TO BUY
ONE RAGS FOR SALE DAUGHTER,
BEFORE WE TOSS HER FOR SALE
INTO THE WATER?"

SPLASH!

Now I'm going down to sea.
Just myself and me.

Just myself and me.
I got my wish
Everyone's gone
except me and my . . .
FISH!

The blue striped grunt,
the rainbow trout,
the catfish and cod
with rhinoceros snout.
They're all swimming over to see.
There's no one here but me.

There's no one here but me,
the largemouth bass,
her big-eyed kids,
a pack of sardines,
and the puckermouth squids.

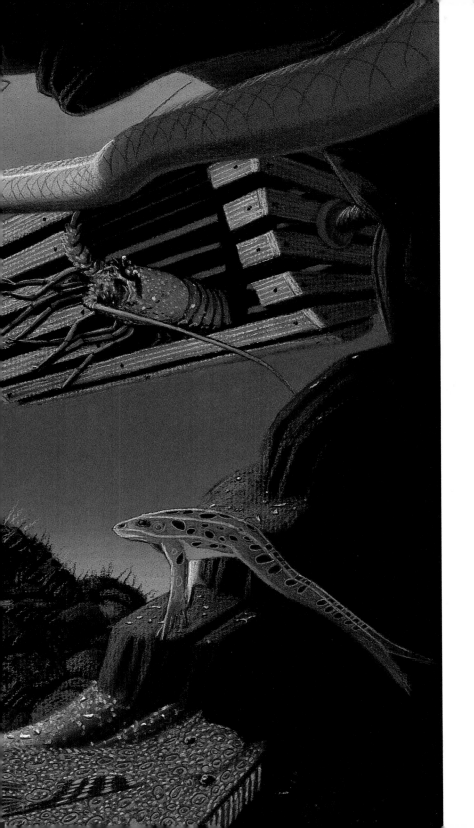

Fish flat as pancakes,
fish that are rounder,
scorpions, snappers,
shrimp, eels, frogs,
and flounder.

Not a person is here
In the world except me . . .

I NEED AIR
I NEED SUN
I NEED MY . . . FAMILY!

So I'll let them all see me
Swim in the water.
RAGS FOR SALE
RAGS FOR SALE
RAGS FOR SALE

DAUGHTER!